Sweepstakes Cop

Michael Slater

authorHOUSE®

AuthorHouse™
1663 Liberty Drive
Bloomington, IN 47403
www.authorhouse.com
Phone: 1-800-839-8640

Published by AuthorHouse   12/16/2016

ISBN: 978-1-4567-5218-7 (sc)
ISBN: 978-1-4567-5404-4 (e)

Library of Congress Control Number: 2011903973

I would like to dedicate this book to the Holy Family, St. Michael who protects all Police Officers & My Guardian Angel who always watched over me!

And

Special Thanks to all the Brave men and women Police Officers who keep the world safe!

Table of Contents

Chapter 1   Hyde Park Paradise 1
Chapter 2   Hyde Park Tree House 3
Chapter 3   Gorilla Lady..7
Chapter 4   Shark Island 11
Chapter 5   Cowgator 13
Chapter 6   Sanddollar Island 17
Chapter 7   Cat Lady and Mr. Henderson....................................19
Chapter 8   Police Career Starts 23
Chapter 9   I Am Free...27
Chapter 10   Discovering Sweepstakes 31
Chapter 11   The Prizes Roll In..33
Chapter 12   Spooky and Close Calls..35
Chapter 13   Too Nice 37
Chapter 14   Patience..39
Chapter 15   Break Dancing 43
Chapter 16   Gazebo..47
Chapter 17   Booby Trap 49
Chapter 18   Stork-it 51
Chapter 19   Karma..53
Chapter 20   Seven Finger Joe..57
Chapter 21   Fight to the Death..59
Chapter 22   The Devil Made Me Do It!...65
Chapter 23   New Year's Eve 67

Chapter One

Hyde Park Paradise

It was the summer of 1972, I had just turned 14 and it was the beginning of a great summer. We had just moved from River Terrace, Florida to a section of Tappan, Florida called Hyde Park.

I was the oldest of five children, three boys and two girls. My sisters; Jill and Cindy were 10 and 12 and my brothers; Jack and Luke were 11 and 13.

My dad's friend's would joke and say, "WOW", your wife has been pregnant for the past five years straight!

My parent's had just purchased a large white two story colonial style home built around 1927. The home was located in the heart of Hyde Park. The house was large around 2900 square feet of charm, character and comfort. It had five bedroom and three bathrooms, a library with a fireplace and a custom built wood table and benches. Outside was a carriage house converted into a small apartment and a two-car garage.

There were several people biding on the home but my parents had the winning bid of $20,000.00. The home came fully furnished including a friendly ghost.

My brothers and I immediately claimed the three upstairs bedrooms and my sisters shared the bedroom downstairs across from our parent's room - which was quite large with two walk-in closets.

Once we settled into our home, my brothers and I went outside to toss a football around. We waved "Hi" to the neighborhood kids who lived across the street and around our age.

The kid's names were Cody and Casey, 12 and 13. Cody also had a sister; Lisa who was 11.

All of us boys became instance friends and little did we know that friendship would carry us through our adult lives.

The next day all of us decided to explore the neighborhood and Cody introduced my brothers and me to Marty and Bobby who were also our same age. We all decided to walk down to the park - which was only one block away. The park had four basketball courts and a small recreation center with ping pong and pool tables.

The neighborhood and park were filled with large majestic grandfather oak trees which towered over the area and sheltering it from the blazing hot Florida sun. The added touch to the area was the nice wide sidewalks with black wrought iron lamp posts.

The park was only four blocks away from Bay Shore Blvd., the world's longest sidewalk -wrapping around the beautiful blue waters of Tappan Bay.

What a sight! It seemed like everyday was a "Beautiful Bay Shore Day".

Life in the 1970's had a magical feel where kids played outside before video games, computers and cell phones came into play.

The pick-up football games, lawn darts, hide and seek seemed like active fun in the remote past. Now kids stay in their bedroom and play video games with kids all over the world without ever leaving their rooms.

But one of my favorite things that I did with my brothers and friends was to build a tree house in the woods behind Cody and Casey's house. There was an eight-acre batch of bamboo woods behind their home we called "Bamboo Forest".

Chapter Two

Hyde Park Tree House

It would take about one day to build my tree house or tree fort what ever you wanted to call it. The tree house was made entirely of scrap wood that I found in the neighborhood.

It would take me about a day to build the tree house and the other guys would take several days if not weeks to build their tree house. The joke was; I was so fast building my tree house that you could sleep in it the same night that I began to build it.

The tree house was high enough off the ground that we could see several blocks away. We felt safe at night and during the day from the neighborhood bullies. We would run an electrical cord from the back of Cody's house through the woods to our tree house. We had a small radio and light so we could see at night.

Another good friend that hung out with us was Tommy who was around 12. When we did spend the night - all the food was supplied by Tommy's father's bakery.

All of our parents never worried about us spending the night. The 70's in Hyde Park were pretty safe and peaceful.

The nights we spent in the tree house were spent walking down the train tracks and always looking for adventure. The train tracks in Hyde Park separated the Caucasian from the African-American homes. It was a Saturday morning around 11:00 am when Cody and his brother Casey, Tommy and I were walking down the train tracks near some heavily wooded - abandoned warehouses, four blocks from our home.

All of us kids being young and dumb didn't know that as we walked down the train tracks we crossed over into a turf that belonged to a group of older African-American teenagers.

The day was going great spending time with my friends until we came across the six older African-American teenagers who were carrying large wood sticks and clubs. The group circled us and the leader of the gang of teenagers said, "We were trespassing on their property and demanded money or they would beat us up."

Cody's brother Casey began to cry, saying that he just got out of the hospital and didn't want to get beaten up. The other guys in my group just looked shocked. The gang kept poking us in our sides with their sticks and clubs.

Just then something within me snapped - since I was the oldest of the group and was always protecting my own brothers and sisters. I yelled at the gang leader to let my friends go and I will give them money and they can beat me up instead. Well I didn't need to say it twice since my friends ran away very quickly. The gang circled me and began jabbing my sides with their sticks and clubs while they began pushing me towards a large patch of woods.

In my mind I knew there was no way that I could run away but I was going to get a few good punches in before they robbed me. It seemed like time was moving in slow motion. The gang wanted me in the woods so no one could see them beating and robbing me.

On the edge of the woods I looked down the train tracks and could not believe what I saw running towards my location. It was my friends returning with their pets which included a very large boa constrictor stretched over Cody's shoulders. Casey was running with a large female german shepherd named Petunia and Tommy was running with a smaller mixed breed named Skipper with a bad attitude and was acting quite brave with Petunia running by his side.

The leader of the gang saw my friends and their pets and knew it was time to run away with his gang members.

It was Cody's idea to get the pets and come back to save me. Cody told me these very wise words. "Friends don't abandon friends when they need your help". Those words are something I will always remember.

After that situation my friends and I decided to turn the unused two car garage into a wrestling ring since we all needed practice getting into shape and defending ourselves.

4

My friends would get a kick out of watching my dad looking at the old black and white T.V. program of local wrestling shows. My dad would ball his fists up and grunt like he was in the wrestling ring himself and throw punches in the air. It was quite funny to watch.

Chapter Three

Gorilla Lady

Living in Florida, we never really had a change of seasons but you could feel and smell the cool October northern air as it gently embraced your face and senses.

Towards the end of October we were all ready for Halloween, the Sunshine State Fair and Buccaneer days filled with historic Pirate festivals. There is also a large wooden Pirate ship carrying around 700 to 800 Pirates. The Pirates capture the city and the whole day is filled with parties and the famous Pirates parade.

When Halloween came we made our own costumes and we all went as a gang of Pirates ourselves. We would go trick or treating through the neighborhood. Everything was so much fun. We would make it safely back home with our candy even though we were chased many times by bullies trying to steal our candy and weirdo's trying to get us into their cars or homes. Our Halloween bags were the large paper grocery bags which would be filled with every type of candy. Our treats would last us for weeks.

The Sunshine State Fair had finally come to Tappan. It was set up at the Tappan University, six blocks from Hyde Park. Around five of my friends and I decided to attend the fair on Saturday evening around 7 pm. We took a short cut down the train tracks and because of the past problems with bullies and pedophiles we filled our pockets with rocks for protection.

In the mid 1970's freak shows still existed and the fair's carnival atmosphere was an amazing event. All my friends wanted to go in so many directions but one of the first freak shows that we went into was the "Woman who turns into a Gorilla."

After paying our money we went inside the large old tent that looked like something out of a World War II encampment. There was saw dust on the floor and around sixty wooden folding chairs in neat rows with thirty chairs on each side of the room and a walkway down the center. Most of the chairs were filled and my friends filled the left over empty chairs in the back. I was left with a chair in the front row which made me feel very uncomfortable.

The show started about ten minutes after we arrived. An older white male in his 60's dressed in a 1920's style jungle safari outfit complete with a safari hat came out from behind a dark burgundy curtain and began to speak. I really began to get nervous because the lights inside the tent went dim and the tone of the man's voice was very spooky as he told his story of a safari in the most dangerous part of unexplored Africa. The man explained that in one of the villages that he came across, a tribe of natives had captured a gorilla that could turn into a beautiful woman.

After the man finished the story his female assistants pulled away the curtain to reveal a beautiful woman around twenty eight years old with dark flowing hair and dressed in a beige outfit sitting in a large chair. At this point I figured the five dollar admission fee that I paid was a rip off and this was a phony show.

One of the assistants began to play some classical music which was very soothing and I could not believe my eyes, somehow the woman did begin turning into a gorilla. I began to get a little nervous as the woman continued to turn into the gorilla. Then after a few minutes the woman had completely turned into a full grown 6'5", 400 lb. Gorilla!!!!

I must have had an out-of-body experience because I immediately jumped up and yelled --- run for your life --- after the gorilla stood up and jumped in front of my seat. I caused a stampede! The audience took off running, turning over chairs and several adults completely ran over me. I kept thinking the gorilla was going to grab me and bite me.

After a few minutes which seemed an eternity I finally was able to get out of the tent. I never looked back and ran all the way home and saw several of my friends were running very quickly in front of me on the train tracks. To this day I have no idea how they did the optical illusion to turn a beautiful woman into a mean looking gorilla.

My friends later said, "It was my fault for causing the stampede" which caused me much embarrassment not to even mention the bruises from being run over by the adults. It was horrifying, but fun at the same time.

Next morning Cody's mom was making breakfast for her family and my brothers and I, when Cody and Jack got this idea to throw some rotten duck eggs - which had been outside for several weeks into the fireplace. Well the eggs exploded and filled the house with a cloud of horrible funky smell causing everyone in the house to run out of the house very quickly. It was very funny to see everyone running out of the house and even Cody's poor dad Mr. Styles who was in a wheelchair. I've never seen Mr. Styles wheel his wheel chair out so quickly down the ramp out of the house as he was yelling Cody's and Jack's name at the same time. Both Cody and Jack were punished. They had to do yard work and volunteer at the local church. Several years later we all laughed including Mr. Styles who thought it was a gas leak and the home was going to explode.

It was in that same time frame when Cody also lost his boa constrictor some where in his house and it turned up between the sheets of their king size bed in Mr. and Mrs. Styles master bedroom.

Lucky for Cody, his Mom had a good sense of humor and just yelled to get the snake out of the bedroom. The snake's name was Joey and he was very friendly but knew how to climb out of his cage and liked to explore Cody's house.

Chapter Four

Shark Island

Our next adventure was going to Palm Tree Island beach which was located about seven miles from Hyde Park in the Port Tappan area. We all caught a ride from Cody's mom Mrs. Styles who was so nice to take us on our adventures with her old blue station wagon she named "Blue Breeze".

Our gang of six friends included Cody and his brother Casey and my brothers and I plus fearless Tommy. We arrived at the beach around 10:00 am on a Saturday morning. We unloaded all of our supplies on the beach - which included two rafts made out of truck inter-tubes, with plywood boards strapped on top plus our coolers filled with food and water.

We pushed the rafts into the water and we set sail pulling our rafts as we swam towards "Sea Gull" island - which seemed like less than one mile away. After about a half an hour we got caught in the current and were drifting towards some channel markers. We were going away from the island instead of getting closer.

I didn't see any shark shows yet but, I was still a little paranoid about sharks. I was laying on one raft, Luke was laying on the other raft and the other four guys were in the water playing with the channel marker. It was a beautiful clear day and the sun was not too hot, so things were looking pretty good until I saw a large gray fin sticking out of the water gliding towards my friends. I started to yell at the guys to get out of the water and they just laughed and thought I was joking until they saw the fin - which was about a 100 yards away from them.

Once all the guys got onto the rafts they began to scream for help, then they saw a second large gray fin come close to the raft that Luke was on. Meanwhile everyone had their legs and arms in the air and only their backs were on the rafts so nothing was in the water. The guys kept screaming and I said, "Don't scream, the hot chicks on the beach will think we are wimps."

Luckily a park ranger spotted us through his binoculars and sent a patrol boat to pick us up. Once the boat came close we all quickly got on the boat and left the rafts which floated away. The park ranger told us that island we were attempting to swim was called, "Shark Island" because of all the sharks in the area.

Chapter Five

Cowgator

Cody's dad Mr. Styles helped all of us guys join the scouts and we thought it would be good for us city kids to venture out into the woods and be able to go camping.

The first meeting for the boy scouts - Mr. Styles took us in his 1965 yellow four door sedan he called "Yellow Fellow" and the cool car doors opened backwards so Mr. Styles was able to slide his wheel chair in with no problem.

Once we got to the meeting for the teenage scouts, we all realized there was a lot of work to gain rank for the scouts and a lot of boring assignments, for us it was like chores. So if the only rank we could obtain is Path Finder - that was okay with us - as long as we could go camping which we did two weeks later after joining the teenage scouts.

Our first camping trip started off on a cool October Friday night. All of the scouts were loaded on the school bus and there was a large trailer being towed behind with our camping supplies. It took about one hour to arrive at the campsite. Once we arrived we were told to set up our tents which we did very quickly. It was very obvious - which scouts came from wealthy families and which scouts came from middle and lower class families. We didn't care we were happy anyway. Once we set up all the camp sights, my friends and I started walking around the different other camp sights, we saw all the really nice tents and delicious food like T-bone steaks on the fire pits in the rich kid's camp area.

Our tents and the food we brought were very humble. I had to laugh because Casey only brought a bag of apples to survive on for the whole weekend. When it came down to cooking dinner, we put all our food together and we called it "HOBO Stew" and it was quite good.

At around 9:00 pm a council meeting was called for everyone to sit around the large bonfire which the adult camp leaders built. The scout's leaders talked about the next day's events and after all the serious matters were discussed the topic changed to ghost stories. One of the first ghost stories had to do with a beast that still roams the area and we all were told to be careful not to explore the areas by ourselves. The beast was called a "Cow-Gator." The beast had the head, tail and feet of an alligator and the large body and legs of a cow.

After about an hour or so of the scary stories it was around 10:30 pm, we still had time to explore before we were required to turn lights out and go to sleep. My friends and I decided to play capture the flag. There were around ten scouts on both sides and each side attempted to steal the other's team flags which were hidden.

The first team to capture the other team's flag was a winner. We used bath towels to represent the flags. One of the scout leaders blew a whistle and the hunt was on to find the other team's flag. The area we were looking for the flag was very dark and I climbed around some very thorny and prickly bushes towards the top of a large hill. I climbed down the hill by myself on the opposite side while looking down at the river which flows near the base of the hill.

While looking for the other team's flag, something suddenly grabbed me and bit my right leg – it wouldn't let me go. I was in a state-of-panic and picked up a tree branch and started to hit the area where the unknown creature was attempting to drag me into the water. It was very dark; I was unable to see anything.

The unknown creature finally let go and I ran in a horrified pace up the top of the hill past my friends, then I ran down the opposite side of the hill towards the adult leaders campsite bouncing off trees all the way down the hill. My friends that I ran past came running down very quickly also - for when they saw the sheer terror in my face and screaming monster the whole time I was running - they did not want this creature that was chasing me to get them.

The scout leaders went down to the area where I was attacked and they saw the drag marks in the dirt by the water and the scout leaders said, "It could have been anything." I showed them my bite marks on my right leg and they didn't believe me since I had cuts all over my body running into trees and thorny bushes. To this day I still have the bit marks and I have no idea what attacked me? Cowgator, Bigfoot who knows? I do know that the capture the flag game was called off - since the leaders were worried that someone could get hurt in the darkness.

Once we arrived home all my friends went up to our tree house and we were watching our little black & white T.V. when Tommy climbed into the tree house with a paper bag filled with vintage nudie magazines. Tommy found the magazines while moving some boxes in the garage. The magazines were from the 1960's and mainly showed a boob or two so we were very happy, but when you're young teenagers' it's great.

So as we were all looking at the magazines, I could hear my mother calling me. Then Tommy's mom started hitting her Chinese gong then Cody's mom began to whistle for him. It was dinner time and my mom is an excellent cook. But just before we took off we decided to bury the magazines in plastic bags in several holes in the bamboo forest. We didn't make it back to the tree house for several days because of the rain but when we did make it back we forgot the location of where we hid the magazines. To this day I am sure the magazines are still out there.

Chapter Six

Sanddollar Island

On Friday the day after Thanksgiving, Tommy borrowed his dad's boat and invited Cody, Casey, Luke, Frankie and I to take the boat out to Sanddollar Island and we thought it would be a lot of fun. So we loaded up the 18 foot fishing boat with supplies and beer we got from Frankie's dad who did not know we were taking them. Everything was going great and since Tommy knew exactly where the Island was located, we got there quickly through the thick fog and dark night.

Once on the Island, Tommy and Frankie decided since we were staying the entire weekend we needed more food. So Tommy and Frankie left the Island around 3:00 am and said, "They would return quickly with the additional food."

Cody and his brother Casey along with my brother Luke and I stayed on the Island and made a small fire, it was cold and the wind was whipping around us. Luke passed the blankets out to us that were kept in a waterproof bag and we all grabbed a spot around the campfire to stay warm. Within fifteen minutes we were all asleep and I was awakened by the sound of Cody yelling that his tennis shoe had caught on fire - he had slept too close to the campfire. We quickly put the fire out and Cody was not injured but it sure was funny to see him hopping around and yelling at the top of his lungs with his tennis shoe on fire.

By this time it was close to daybreak, maybe 6:00 am and Frankie and Tommy had not returned from getting supplies. We were getting concerned since the only food and drinks we had was a case of warm beer and several dozen bait shrimp. By noon Frankie and Tommy never showed up and we were very hungry so we started searching the Island for anything to eat.

Cody & Casey went one way and Luke and I went the opposite way. The only thing we found to eat was oysters in some shallow water. So we cooked the oysters and bait shrimp we had for fishing. Later that day we caught Luke with a candy bar, chewing away looking like he was really enjoying himself.

By day two we were starving and I decided to take the BB gun we brought and hunt for seagulls thinking they would taste like chicken. I came very close but no seagull dinner.

On day three our friends finally came back. They were being towed by another boat to the island to pick us up. After Tommy and Frankie had left the island they were speeding along in the boat when they hit an oyster bed and it sheared off the propeller, they became stranded in the bay and floated several miles into the Gulf of Mexico. They attempted to paddle with the water ski but it wasn't helping. To make matters worse, no one was stopping to help and they survived on potato chips and cokes. Finally a passing boat captain was nice to stop for them on day three and towed the boat to the island and then back to shore.

I think the worst thing about the whole situation was that my fellow students found out at school and I was called, "Sea Gull Eater," I would just laugh.

Chapter Seven

Cat Lady and Mr. Henderson

I learned a lot from my dad about saving money when you have a big family. One of the things my dad would do is bring all of his dress white shirts to a lady who would clean and starch them for 10 cents a piece. One day my dad asked me to go along with him to pick up his shirts which I did.

We knocked on the front door and a very friendly woman in her 50's opened the door and let us in - but as soon as the door opened I thought I was going to die from the cat-urine-fumes.

I didn't want to go in but when the lady and my dad invited me I couldn't refuse. There must have been at least 30 to 40 cats of all sizes and shapes. As I walked around, I left footprints in the green shag carpeting due to the fact the carpeting was soaked with cat-urine, how gross and disgusting, I felt like I was going to throw up.

Once we got outside my dad went into the car trunk and pulled out a can of deodorizer and sprayed the shirts to kill the cat-urine-smell. As we were driving home my dad began to have an evil type laugh and said, "When I am at work in the office and my shirts begin to smell from the cat-urine, I just blame is on who ever is sitting next to me."

"Oh! The childhood memories"

Once we got home our next door neighbor approached us and wanted to talk. My dad was in a hurry to go inside so I stayed outside and listened to Henry. Henry was a kind older man in his late 70's, a lonely widower. He didn't have any family so I would listen to his interesting stories. One day Henry told me about the people that use to live in our house. They were the Henderson's and they lived at the house for over 40 years until they both died.

Each night Mr. Henderson would go drinking around 9:00 pm and would come home around 1:00 am intoxicated. One night while Mr. Henderson was intoxicated, he stumbled as he was climbing up the stairs to the second floor, fell and broke his neck. Mrs. Henderson died several years later from a broken heart. So the house was put up for sale and since the Henderson's family lived in New York, all the furniture was sold with the house.

The rumor was that somewhere in the house Mr. Henderson buried his fortune that he made off his family business. I asked Henry where he thought the money was and he said, "It could be under the house or several other hiding places that Mr. Henderson was known to hide things."

He recalled that one day Mr. Henderson did get hurt by falling off the ladder in the upstairs hall closet while repairing a hole in the wall he was fixing. For me, this cleared up many questions like; why each night around 1:00 am I would hear footsteps climbing the wood steps leading up to the second floor.

Once the ghost or spirit reached the second floor it would walk to the first room and push open the door and climb into bed which unfortunately was my bed. After the first week of scaring the crap-out-of- me, I would just figure it was the harmless, friendly ghost of Mr. Henderson.

A rumor got started at school that we had a ghost and I decided to make some money off the situation. So I would bet kids at school that they couldn't spend the whole night in the first upstairs bedroom.

My parents thought that I had so many friends because each weekend someone new would try to spend the night and around 1:30 am they would normally run out of the house extremely frighten. Some of the kids would say the ghost would touch their toes, some would say the ghost touched their hair. All I knew that it was fun making money with my pal - Mr. Henderson.

My father didn't believe in ghosts until one day he was alone in the house and said, "The front door would open, then it would close, he would then lock it. Then the back door would open, then it would close, he would then lock that one." I know Mr. Henderson was having fun that day.

I got along with all my brothers and sisters, except at times, my brother Jack - who was only 14 months younger than me. It would only take the wrong word for me to say and he would wrestle me to the ground. I was bigger and stronger and would just hold him down until he cooled off. Little did he know at the time, but he was helping me. All this fighting experience would be helpful in my future police career - when criminals would attack me.

My friends laugh to this day about all the times Jack and I would get in a wrestling match and he would tell people he was the older brother. I would think to myself if that makes him happy "good" whatever it takes to keep the peace with my brother.

Chapter Eight

Police Career Starts

After high school graduation and spending four years in the Army I went after my dream job of becoming a police officer. I never realized it would be so much fun and tough at the same time.

Learning so much about all different levels of law and being able to get into the best shape of my life. My police recruit class started off with 40 men and women and in the final week the class was down to just 20 men and women. One of the final physical training exams was running a mile in eight minutes and if you were not able to complete this final test - you could not graduate from the Police Academy.

Since I was fast, I thought it would be no problem completing this run. The day we ran was Thursday around 7:30 am - on a hot and humid summer morning. The run was on an old dirt road with heavy woods on both sides. There were instructors at the starting and finishing line and on both sides of the road to make sure everyone finished and didn't cheat.

At the start of the race it seemed like it was going to be a three-man race since my two friends and I were leading everyone else. My other two friends, Ray who was a tall African-American guy was on my high school football team. J.T., a shorter African-American guy had the funniest sense of humor and helped me study for the police exam.

Ray was leading and J.T. was in second and I was in third leaving everyone far behind. I was halfway through when it hit me, I had to go to the bathroom and I'm sure it was diarrhea from something I ate for breakfast. As I'm running, I yelled to one of the instructors, I've got to go to the bathroom and the instructor order me to finish the race or get fired.

I made a decision to jump out of the race into the woods right near one of the instructors so that he wouldn't think I was cheating, I went to the bathroom, jumped back into the race and caught up with my two friends and still finished third in a race of 20 people.

The instructors still talk about that race to this day and if Slater can jump out of race, jump back into the race and finish third - then everyone should be able to finish. So my police career started off with the nick name; "Flash."

My first shift was the night shift - which was 11:00 pm to 7:00 am. I rode with a training officer for the first two months. The more experienced officer teaches proper traffic stops, police call procedures and does written evaluations on the trainee who was me.

Within the first hour around 12:00 am my training partner and I received a call about an unknown person deceased under a bridge near downtown. Upon our arrival there were several police vehicles as well as a crime scene unit. My training partner; Gus said, "Mike you have to check this out." There was this large crack at the base of this abandoned building where homeless people would climb through and sleep in the basement of the building. An older white male around 55 years old had been drinking; he had fallen backwards and hit his head on a cement block. Once he was knocked out, there were very large rats eating the meat from his legs, arms and face. What was left over looked like something out of a Wax Museum. You really feel sadness for the homeless man.

The rest of the time spent with the training officer that evening was quiet and our shift ended without incidents. On my last day of riding with Gus it was about 3:00 am and we were driving on the interstate near downtown. When I noticed a dark lump that looked like a dog with some type of cloth wrapped around it. Gus yelled at me to pull over to the shoulder of the road which I did very quickly. We got out and Gus said, "That's no dog - it is a young women."

It was really a sad sight to see the poor woman. We called for back-up to block off the interstate so we could do an investigation. We were able to find out that the woman's name was Anna and she was having problems with her boyfriend. After questioning the boyfriend, he finally confessed. The boyfriend, John R. stated that while driving with his girlfriend – they got into an argument; he opened the door and kicked Anna out of the speeding car into the dark interstate road. Anna's body was struck numerous times by passing vehicles and ended up on the shoulder of the road. Several days later I saw flowers where Anna's body was found and John R. was given life in prison.

Chapter Nine

I Am Free

Yes, my first day by myself was so much fun. When I was driving on an isolated section of the city with no other traffic around, I turned on my lights and siren - what a rush.

Some older officers wanted me to back them up so they could catch some drug dealers. There were three police cars with five police officers including myself. We pulled up quickly to the location of the drug dealers and they began to run away. All the police officers and I started chasing the suspects through the woods and I finally caught up with three of the drug dealer suspects as they were scrabbling up a hill. I turned around and realized that I was all alone so I grabbed two of the suspects and bluffed them to give up without a fight because they were surrounded. I marched the two suspects back to my police car and the other police officers apologized for not keeping up and I said, "I will take the credit for arresting the two dealers and 50 pieces of crack."

All that running in the police academy paid off. I had a different outlook on police work than some of the guys on the force. My mother raised me to respect and have compassion for all people.

After probation I was assigned to zone 4 on the 3:00 to 11:00 pm shift. My shift sergeant asked me to take care of a problem with some gang members that were bothering local citizens. The problem was on 34th and 35th street in the west-end area of the city. A group of 10 or more African-American gang members were hanging outside of a neighborhood grocery store harassing all the customers coming near the store. Since the neighborhood had many elderly people living in the area, they had no other grocery store to count on. Another police officer named Larson told me, good luck. No other police officer was able to take care of the problem and other cops didn't want the headache.

As a young kid I would watch a weekly T.V. show about a small town sheriff who always handled the toughest situations without ever using his gun. I guess you could say that sheriff was my role model.

So I drove up to the area where the gang was hanging out and I got out of my police car without ever saying a word, the group circled me quickly and started yelling - calling me "Honky Pig, get out of here." I didn't say a word; instead I was counting the gang members with my index finger. Then the leader of the gang came up to me and said, "What are you counting?"

Then I calmly said, "I'm trying to figure out how many people I need to arrest to buy a new stereo system." The gang leader then said, "What do you mean?" Let me explain myself, each person I arrest is worth an extra $75.oo added into my paycheck, since I have to attend court and get paid for three hours overtime.

After hearing what I said, the gang leader yelled; "It's not worth going to jail" - they didn't just walk away - they ran away, all ten of them.

As I was talking with them I guess some local citizen called the police department when they witnessed the gang had circled me and the citizen must have thought I was in danger. Several police cars showed up to my location and saw the gang members running away. Some of the police officers wondered how I took care of resolving the problem; of gang members terrorizing the neighborhood for the last eight years. I told the guys I simply reasoned with them. Several senior citizens came out of their homes and began clapping - for getting rid of the gang problem. Even my unit sergeant wanted me to tell the other police officers at roll call how I took care of the problem.

A week later I saw a fellow police officer chasing a car thief down an alley yelling at the thief to stop - saying he needed money for a toaster oven so stop running. That was very funny and he did catch the car thief.

Two weeks later on a busy Friday night around ll:00 pm, a fellow police officer named Joe was calling over the police radio for help. I arrived within minutes and Joe said, "There were two burglars breaking into the liquor store and I got one of the burglars in the back of my police car and the other one escaped. The other burglar ran across the four lane road into a thick patch of woods which was around 2 to 3 acres. The whole area was very dark and several other police officers came on the scene to assist. I told the other police officers that the suspect was in the woods and let's go get him. The other two police officers just looked at me and said, "We are not going into the woods and get killed over looking for a burglary suspect who might have a gun."

So being young and dumb with no fear - I decided to go into the woods by myself. I took several steps into the woods and then got on my hands and knees and began to make weird animal noise like a raccoon with rabies. I figured the burglary suspect would be scared in the dark woods. My plan worked because the burglary suspect began to make noise by moving around as he lay by a log. My eyes adjusted to the darkness and I spotted the suspect hiding by a fallen tree, he was laying parallel by the tree.

The suspect was an African-American male around mid-thirty's 225 lbs and around 6'2" wearing a beige knit cap, blue jeans and blue shirt. I moved very slowly towards the suspect then jumped on his back and I began to wrestle with him. The suspect was very strong and I think he must have thought I was an animal because he was screaming for help.

The other police officers outside the woods thought it must have been me screaming for help because they called for additional police officers, a helicopter and the K9 unit. I finally got the suspect handcuffed; we were both covered with mud. I was able to drag the suspect out of the woods to the clearing where all the other police officers were located. The helicopter shined the spot light on the suspect as we walked out. I heard one of the police officers at the scene yelled with Slater you don't need police dogs.

Chapter Ten

Discovering Sweepstakes

Police work has moments of quick excitement and long periods of sheer boredom which is good. That means crime is slowing down and I would get stuck on stakeouts needing something to read. So I read a magazine about entering sweepstakes and I ordered a subscription to the sweepstakes contest magazine. It has hundreds of companies giving things away to promote and advertise their product.

I would normally work the graveyard shift - 12 to 8:00 am - which was nice to see the city go to sleep and then rise up each day with the sunrise.

When things started to slow down around 4 am, I would stop in an isolated area and begin to do my sweepstakes. I would flip through the magazine and see what prizes I would like to win. Several other police officers saw me doing this same routine every night and they thought I was doing paperwork - which I didn't mind staying at one spot for a long period of time.

My supervisors volunteered me any time there was a stakeout of any kind or guarding a prisoner in a hospital, anything else that require a police officer to stay at one location for long periods of time. The other police officers hated staying at one location for long periods and would also volunteer my name by saying, "Slater likes it!"

What no one understood was that I was entering sweepstakes of all kinds and winning prizes of everything you could imagine. I was also a deeply religious man of faith and would pray the rosary after I finished doing my sweepstakes each night. With my investigation skills I was able to determine what sweepstakes I had the best chance on winning, what post office would get my mail the quickest and how I was going to decorate my envelopes; a colorful beach or mountain scenery.

One night I was guarding a prisoner in a local hospital and around 1:30 while drawing a beach scene on one of my envelopes, several nurses walked by and laughed at the macho cop decorating the envelopes. My theory was the people that worked at these sweepstake headquarters get bored and I would cheer them up by decorating them and putting "Have a nice day" and other cheerful or funny salutations.

Chapter Eleven

The Prizes Roll In

The prizes really began to take off, I won a pick-up truck from a local news station, won a trip for two to South West Texas from a potato chip company - had a cook-out with a beautiful country singer. I attended the All-Bowl in Hawaii which was also amazing. I kicked field goals at the Grand Tarpon football stadium at a chance to win airline tickets. I was a grand prize winner of a razor blade company who gave me $10,000.00 and a trip to the Caribbean Islands for a week of scuba diving. I passed footballs at a moving golf cart at the University of Tappan stadium for prizes. Pretty much if you could name it I probably won it, but not in my wildest dreams did I ever know what major prize was headed my way.

I was good friends with all the convenience clerks and one of the clerks gave me the nick name, "Sweepstakes Cop" which stuck with me to this day.

I was always on treasure hunts looking for new sweepstakes. I did get negative feedback from family and friends who thought I was wasting my time and money.

Chapter Twelve

Spooky and Close Calls

As I did my sweepstakes every night, I would listen to a radio talk show about UFO's and ghost stories, it was very interesting.

I can still remember the story that a police instructor; Officer Roberts once told my class at the police academy. He answered a call from a person at a large and very spooky looking home. Upon his arrival he spoke with an elderly woman in her eighty's - who invited him into her home. Officer Roberts followed the woman down a hallway and as he was walking he glanced into a room with an open door and saw a woman with no legs and no arms thrust herself out of her bed onto the floor. Upon seeing this, Officer Roberts quickly ran out of the house. Officer Roberts was very embarrassed and figured he had watch one too many horror movies and strongly recommended to all of us not to fill our minds with anything negative. Officer Roberts did go back into the house and apologized to the elderly woman and said, "He had to answer a call."

Chapter Thirteen

Too Nice

I know being a police officer is my destiny and everything in my life added up to this career. I came to work one day and an older police officer who had been on the job for more than 20 years told me that I was too nice to the citizens on the street. Officer Jenkins then went onto say my niceness is a sign of weakness. I told Jenkins that I'm here to protect and serve not to harass and intimidate. I had my own style that if I treated people with respect - that I would get respect in return. My grandmother once told me that a smile and a kind word is a powerful message.

It got back to my supervisors from some of my fellow officers that I was too soft on citizens and that I needed to learn how to be a tougher cop. So I was given an assignment of walking a foot beat by myself between 1:00 am and 4:00 am. It was one of the most dangerous housing projects - where just recently a police officer was shot and killed.

Co-worker Officer James dropped me off and said, "Good Luck!" I got out of the police car and Officer James drove off quickly. There were about 8 to 10 African-America male gang members on each side of the street. The two separate gangs walked toward my location and I told them it was their lucky day because I was calling a truce and was going to take their complaints to the Mayor of the city. I told both gang leaders, I need a list of demands and complaints. One gang member told me I've got "Elephant Balls" for coming by myself and I told him I was on a "Mission from Jesus" - they started to laugh and invited me for a cook out at one of the gangs clubs. The gang members set up chairs and fired up the barbeque and cranked up the music and the party was on!

After speaking with both gang members they realized that they had a lot in common and arguing didn't make sense.

I told them it was their responsibility to protect the women and children from violence. They all agreed and asked me why the other cops were so mean and I told them I'm sure it was a big misunderstanding. Meanwhile one of my supervisors told Officer James to pick me up from the projects. When Officer James came to the area where I was, he called me on my police radio numerous times and I was unable to hear him - due to fact that the stereo was so loud. Officer James told my supervisor of the situation and he sent all available police cars to find me in the projects. I'm sure they thought I was dead somewhere in the area. I think when they found me they must have had 15 to 20 police cars looking for me. I finally looked at my watch and thanked the gang members and started walking to the spot where my fellow officers were going to pick me up. I think four or five police cars came zooming up to my location and my fellow police officers jumped out of their cars and were just shocked to see me alive.

Several days later at around 2:00 am, I was patrolling the same project when I saw a drug deal going down and went to investigate. Instead of the drug dealers running away when they saw me, the two drugs dealers started coming toward me - they had a look on their face that they were going to attack so I was getting ready to pull my gun. Then I heard a loud yell, I stopped, the drug dealers stopped and a group of residents from the projects came running and surrounded me telling the drug dealers that I was their friend and to leave me alone - they left the area immediately.

"WOW," I know my Guardian Angel was working overtime the last couple of days.

Chapter Fourteen

Patience

The following morning around 8:00 am I was notified that I would be working an extra shift on the daylight from 8:00 am to 4:00 pm.

Being a Saturday morning, I decided to get a cup of coffee at the local gas station to try to stay awake - since I was so tired from working the night before. Upon my arrival at the gas station I noticed a small red colored vehicle with a license plate that I had been looking for - for several days. The driver matched the description of the robber who robbed the video store. The car was parked in the rear of the gas station and the driver was getting out of his car. Once the driver saw me he jumped back into his car and drove out of the gas station parking lot. I quickly followed the suspect who was a white male in his mid 20's, close to my age, wearing a brown baseball cap. I was about one car length behind the suspect as we both drove north on the main highway. I tried to stay far enough behind the suspect so he did not get suspicious.

I called for back-up to assist me making the arrest in case he was armed and there was a shootout in the area. After a half mile of following the suspect I saw the suspect take off his baseball hat and slam it several times on the front passenger seat. At this point, back-up had not arrived and I did not want the suspect to do something crazy so I changed lanes and drove past his car. The suspect quickly made a hard right turn and pulled into the local hamburger restaurant parking lot. I also made a hard right turn and drove my police car into the opposite side of the hamburger restaurant parking lot. I quickly exited my police car and was going to run through the hamburger restaurant to get the suspect on the other side. As I entered the restaurant to my surprise, the suspect was inside robbing the restaurant as the customers lay on the floor. The suspect had his back to me pointing a 38 caliber handgun at the manager - who had his arms raised in the air slightly shaking.

Not to surprise the robber by yelling police, because I didn't want him shooting anyone. I called out John what are you doing? The robber turned his head slightly towards me while keeping the handgun pointed at the manager. To his disbelief he saw me with my gun pointing at him and I repeated to the suspect, look John you are just having a bad day - just slide the gun over to me so we can talk about high school football glory days. The robbery suspect kept yelling at me that his name was not John and he would shoot the manager. I said, "John, you were very cool in high school and as your friend, I feel your pain and I will help you."

Meanwhile the restaurant customers and manager looked at me like I was crazy and of all the police officers - why did we have to get this one. But my unorthodox method did work and the suspect slid his gun over towards me and I simply put the handcuffs on him, padded him on the back and said, "It's going to be okay." Just then, my back-up came driving into the restaurant parking lot with sirens blaring and charging towards my direction with their guns drawn.

I told my fellow officers thanks, but the situation was under control. I put the suspect in the paddy wagon and drove to the police station to do my paperwork. One of the guys at the station yelled at me to pickup the phone - which I did and spoke to a Mr. Larson. He said, "I want to thank you for saving my son's life in the restaurant." I asked Mr. Larson if his son was one of the customers. He replied that his son was the person robbing the restaurant. Mr. Larson went onto say that his son has a drug problem and by me taking the time and talking with him instead of shooting him, he gets another chance for having a good relationship with his son.

I thought that it was pretty cool how things worked out - since the local chamber of commerce gave the guys at the station and I a big party. I caught a lot of flak from the guys for being a big hero but it's something I will always remember. I have no clue where the idea came from except that 1960's comedy shows about a deputy sheriff who always solved the crime without using any type of deadly force.

I thanked my "Guardian Angel" for helping me but I'm sure he or she must wish they were assigned to a more peaceful person instead of all the action I get into daily.

Chapter Fifteen

Break Dancing

Working the graveyard shift was really nice - there was no traffic, the weather was mostly clear and the stars filled the skies.

The trick I had for riding alone in my police car was to hang a hat above the passenger seat head rest. Then I would drape a raincoat over it so it looked like a person was riding with me. At night it was so dark, all you could see is a large object that looked like a person

I would always say to any suspects that were going to get violent, don't make my grumpy partner get out of the car because he was working out at the gym today and is still pumped up from the steroids he took. Most of the time the suspects would just look at my car and say damn I don't want that honky jumping out on me. Trust me that little trick worked numerous times when I was out numbered by the bad guys trying to harm me.

A lot of my fellow police officers that I worked with were close to my age of twenty four. When things slowed down at night, police officer would pull their police car's facing each other with their driver's side windows down. This way we could talk to each other and could watch each others backs if one cop was tired - they could rest their eyes for a few minutes.

A number of times when I would meet up with one of the other police officer friends, I would wear some type of horrible monster mask to scare the crap of out of them. One night I responded to an alarm at a Jr. High school. Police radio dispatch stated, that there were several silent alarms going off - so it was a good alarm. That meant that the suspect was still in the building and there was a possibility of more than one suspect.

Upon my arrival I parked my police car several blocks away to make sure the burglars did not see my headlights. I walked around the perimeter of the building checking for any broken glass.

I found a broken window and continued to walk around in the darkness outside the building. I spotted two burglars - who were African-American teenage males, 14 to 15 years old. Each suspect was carrying a small cardboard box and it looked like they were shopping - the way they were examining each item they picked up. I decided that by the time I climbed through the broken window and attempted to catch the youths that it wasn't worth it - since the court system is too lenient on juveniles.

I figured I would do some street justice and I went back to my car and got the monster mask. Then I ran back to the window where the suspects were located. I put the monster mask on and went up to the window and only exposed my face which was covered with the mask. One of the suspects was also acting like a lookout and since it was so dark, I guess he thought he saw me and went up to the window where I was located. As soon as the suspect saw me he collapsed onto the floor. I thought I gave him a heart attack - until I saw him spinning around in a circle looking like he was trying to break dance.

The other suspect was very confused watching his partner in crime spinning on the floor without screaming, I guess he was too scared. The other suspect finally saw me and I growled very loud. Immediately the suspect then threw the box up in the air and screamed and ran out of the room.

I decided to quickly climb through the broken window just in case the other suspect spinning on the floor was hurt in any way. As I was walking down the dark hallway I heard the blood curling sounds of two terrified teenager suspects. I found both pairs of suspect's tennis shoes - where they ran completely out of them. I ran to the door where the suspects exited the building and could still hear the suspects screaming as they ran through the woods away from the school.

I went to the room where the suspects were stealing and found most of the chairs knocked down and a large wet spot where the suspect that was break-dancing must have wet his pants. The suspect's boxes were filled with assorted goodies and ice cream sandwiches that they attempted to steal. I don't think those two suspects will ever attempt to steal anything ever again.

While I'm on the subject of monsters and scary moments, I was driving down a city street in a neighborhood of nice homes and manicured lawns. When all of a sudden a white male around 30 years old came running up to my police car screaming; MONSTERS! MONSTERS!

The suspect told me he was guilty of breaking into a home and saw monsters. I patted the suspect down for weapons and I put him in the back seat and drove to the location to see what's going on? Upon my arrival at the house - where the suspect told me the monsters were hiding, I knocked on the front door of the neatly kept home. I must tell you I was a little spooked since I know how scared the suspect looked and acted. The front door finally opened and a kindly older white gentleman in his 70's asked me what the problem was at this hour of the night - which was around 1:00 am in the morning. As it turned out, both the home owners were legally blind and were having a late night snack in their kitchen which they kept dark - there was no need for lights.

The husband, Mr. Harper did say he heard a noise in the living room like a window opening. Then a few minutes later heard footsteps, and a loud scream - then the front door opened and slammed shut. I went outside and got a statement from the suspect who did say he opened the living room window from the outside, climbed through and was walking down the hallway when he heard scraping and taping noises coming from the kitchen.

Upon a closer look the suspect saw two people sitting with the lights off in the kitchen. I think the suspect saw one too many horror pictures because the suspect thought they were vampires or some type of monsters eating in the dark. The suspect was charged with burglary. I told him the people were blind and it was a lesson to the suspect to give up his life of crime. The suspect reassured me he was giving up drugs and a life of crime.

When I went to court the suspect told me the other prisoner found out what happened and were laughing at him. Suspect said, "He deserved it and apologized to Mr. and Mrs. Harper for breaking into their home and causing them problems."

Chapter Sixteen

Gazebo

Sometimes you just get lucky solving crimes and being in the right place at the right time, like the suspect I call, "Mr. Gazebo."

On a Tuesday morning around 3:30 am, I was driving in a nice middle-class neighborhood when I spotted a white male in his early 20's dressed in all black.

The suspicious person was checking out the rear of a house that had no outside lights on. I quickly stopped my vehicle and turned the headlights off and quietly exited my police car. I advised police radio dispatch of the situation and that I would be turning my police radio off for a few minutes so there would be no noise. Police radio dispatch asked if I needed any back-up and I said, "No, due to the fact it might scare this suspect away." We did have some reported rapes and thefts in the area and the suspect fit the profile and description.

The home owners had a garden gazebo directly next to the house and there was one open window - which the suspect must have seen since he began to climb the gazebo. The suspect was able to climb through the open window after he was on the very top of the gazebo.

I could see from the street that the suspect had a little flashlight and he was moving very slowing in the room. I didn't want to wake the homeowners, as I was worried the suspect might do something to harm them.

So I climbed the gazebo and very quietly climbed through the window where the suspect was stalking around. I caught the suspect off guard and I think I scared the crap-out-of-him. I quickly subdued him in handcuffs.

I began to take the suspect out of the house and was met by the homeowner, Mr. Joe who was in his tee shirt and boxer underwear carrying a golf club standing in the upstairs hallways in disbelief. I told Mr. Joe what happened and I was taking this burglary suspect out of the house to jail and apologized for making noise and waking him up. Mr. Joe just shook his head in disbelief.

I took the suspect to jail and my fellow officers heard what happened and started calling me "Spider Cop". All my supervisors who called me, "Too soft," wanted me to patrol their neighborhoods, since I was lucky catching burglars.

Chapter Seventeen

Booby Trap

I stopped in one of my favorite convenience stores and the clerk Sammy said, "How's the Sweepstakes Cop doing tonight and what have you won lately?"

After about 30 minutes in the store, I bought my stamps, envelopes and coffee. I was on my way driving down Lee highway - when police dispatch gave me a robbery call to the same address of the convenience store that I had just left. I was only a couple of blocks away when I received the call and make a quick u-turn and speeded towards the store and entered the parking lot. I slammed on my brakes and my police car slid towards the front door. Just at that moment an African-American suspect in his 20's came running out of the store with a hand gun in his right hand and a paper bag of money in his left hand. The suspect was dressed in a dark blue jacket and sweat pants. Suspect was around 5' 10" 170 lbs. - I quickly exited the police car and started chasing the suspect who had a 25 yard head start. The rear of the convenience store was very dark, but I spotted the suspect as he was running towards the street away from the store.

Just as the suspect was crossing the street, a small pick-up truck stopped as the suspect ran in front of him. The driver of the pick-up and the passenger got out and began running with the armed robber. The driver and passenger were both African-American males around 20 to 25 years old. I'm thinking what in the world do I have here? The three suspects ran behind some homes and I lost sight of them for several minutes until I heard several loud screams.

The suspects had entered the basement of a home which was under construction and I guess the homeowner was sick of people stealing from him so he set up a booby trap. The booby trap was wooded boards with large nails sticking out of them. The homeowner buried the wood under the dirt, so you couldn't see them. The suspects entered the basement and all three suspects stepped on the boards and were stuck to them when I arrived.

What a sight! It looked very painful. The suspects were taken to the hospital then to jail. The two suspects who had jumped out of the pick-up had just stole the truck and when they saw me running towards their direction, they panicked and fled with the armed robber who they did not even know. The money was returned to the store and the truck was returned to the owner. What a night - A two for one!

Later that morning around 4:00 am, I was driving behind one of the large retailers that sell everything inside and outside the home. In the back of the store, there was a fenced in area where they kept the lawn mowers and lawn furniture. To my surprise there was an African-American male in his 30's who was trying to steal a lawn mower by pulling it all the way to the top of the 10 foot fence. The suspect saw me and dropped the lawn mower then fled into the woods. I didn't chase him, I just laughed! I tried to figure out why climb a 10 foot fence when you could just cut a hole in the fence to take the lawn mower?

Chapter Eighteen

Stork-it

Older cops would say that our police zone was like a violent war zone. From the time I was getting ready for work until the time I went home - there was always calls waiting to be answered. It was so busy; it was hard to get back-up on dangerous calls. You would learn how to handle dangerous police calls by yourself.

My next big call I wouldn't soon forget, because I came very close to dying. I receive this call from a home about a possible stabbing. Upon my arrival, there were two fire trucks parked in front of the home with four firemen standing behind their fire trucks. I exited my police car and the firemen yelled at me to come back over here! So I went to talk with the fire captain and he told me don't go up to the house and where is your back-up officer?

I told the Captain I was by myself since the other officers were busy. The Captain replied don't go up to the house, but would not give me a reason why. I told the Captain, it's my job and I had to answer the call. I started walking up the long concrete sidewalk but just before I got to the front door, which was slightly opened, the door flung open with such tremendous force causing several panels of glass embedded in the door to break. Then a completely naked 300 lb 5'8" African-American woman came charging at me with a large 8 inch butcher knife, screaming die you "Honky Pig." I took several quick steps back, stood in a defensive stance and saw the speed of the woman running at me. I knew there was no chance in using my gun - I would still end up getting stabbed because at that short distance the bullet would not have stopped her.

As a young kid if I was ever charged at by someone - I would do my "Stork-it" so I could trip them before they harmed me. I leaned backwards at the last moment and tripped the woman who had such rage in her eyes; her butcher knife was shining from the street lights.

I worked quickly to put the handcuffs on the woman and got the knife off the grass where it had fallen out of her hand after she tripped. I placed the woman in the back of my car and threw a rain coat over her. The paramedic's check her out for any injuries - which were none except for the scrapes on her legs and arms from tripping on the concrete sidewalk.

As it turned out the woman's name was Thelma and she caught her husband with another women and she had become enraged. The woman that Melvin was with fled quickly, but Melvin was stabbed to death by Thelma. That was the same time I was at the front door and Thelma saw me and tried to kill me as well.

The firemen yelled out "Great Job!" I told the firemen, please let me know what's waiting for me next time behind the door. The Captain didn't know how to say - that a very large and naked woman with a large butcher knife was behind the front door.

Off duty I had a stiff drink and it didn't sink in until a couple of days later. I sometimes have dreams about it.

Chapter Nineteen

Karma

I know everything happens for a reason. The world is like a big bouncing ball. You receive what you give.

A new guy by the name of Jake was only on the police department a few days when he got shot. Unfortunately Jake had accidentally shot himself by mistake. Jake must have thought he was a cowboy in a western-type movie when he was quick drawing in from of a mirror and shot himself in the right leg. My supervisors were getting ready to fire Jake since he was still in his probationary period at the police department. At the last moment one of the supervisors had a change of heart and talked to the other supervisors into letting Jake stay on.

That would be a good thing because two weeks later on an early Saturday morning around 6:30 am. Jake happened to be driving around the building of a large department store, when he saw an older white male around 50 to 60 years old grab a young boy around 5 years old. Jake became suspicious and radioed dispatch for back-up. The unknown male suspect then drove off quickly in a rust colored van. The van was stopped several miles away from the location after receiving back-up from several officers and me who had rushed to the scene.

Jake went to talk with the white male driver and I went to the passenger side of the van and heard a muffled type sound. I quickly opened the sliding door of the van and discovered the small boy who was in handcuffs and had grey colored duck tape over his mouth. At this point the suspect attempted to reach for a handgun in the glove box, but Jake and several other officers wrestled with him and put the handcuffs on him quickly.

I took the tape and handcuffs off the little boy. I asked the boy his name and he replied Matthew. I asked Matthew where is daddy and he told me collecting cans. I went back behind the department store where the boy was kidnapped and found Matthew's dad in the store's dumpster looking for cans. I told Matthew's dad what happened and he explained to me that he was only in the dumpster for a few minutes. He did not know his son was kidnapped by the pedophile. He had a look of sheer terror on his face and took little Matthew home.

All I can say is thank goodness Jake was not fired and was in the right place at the right time!

The next night my first call was for unknown trouble. Upon my arrival, I spoke with Karen T who invited me in her home. Karen T. was carrying a baseball bat and so was her son Spencer. I told them both to put the baseball bats down - that they were safe now. Karen T. asked me if I saw the UFO spaceship above the house before I came in and I replied no. Karen T. told me that there was a space alien in the house somewhere. I began to follow Karen T. around the house and she would point at the rooms and I would go into them and check them out.

One of the rooms that I went into, I got hit in the head with a pillow by Karen T's husband who thought I was his wife. Robert T. yelled get out of my room you crazy bitch and stop waking me up. I just laughed and closed the door. I advised Karen T. the house was safe, for her and her son Spencer to go to bed.

I left the house and began to drive down an old abandoned roadway looking for a good location to do my sweepstakes. Then out of no where came this bright light and was hovering over my police car as I drove down the roadway. All my locked doors started to pop up and down and that freaked me out. I pulled over and jumped out of the car. The bright light then flew away. I then realized that I was locked out of my police car and notified radio dispatch to send a tow truck over to unlock my car door.

My supervisor heard what was going on and said, "He was coming to my location with a spare key and cancel the tow truck." The supervisor, Sgt. Bill had a very angry tone to his voice and I knew I was in trouble. Once Sgt. Bill arrived at the scene he began to yell at me for not being careful and I tried to explain what happened. Sgt. Bill said, "Excuses!"

then Sgt. Bill gave me the car keys and I opened the door and gave them back to the Sergeant.

Then out of no where the bright light came back and began hovering over our heads and the Sergeant screamed what the hell! It seemed like our electronic systems and door locks began to act crazy like before. The sergeant yelled at me to get into my police car, drive away and not to tell anyone about the UFO. I asked the sergeant, "Do you believe me now?" He just said, "Shut up and let's get out of here and we did." The bright light flew away as we drove away.

The sergeant was worried that people would think we were both crazy. So this is the first time I have ever talked about this to anyone. I won't laugh at anyone who says they spotted a UFO now, I am now a believer. Needless to say I won't do any more sweepstakes in that area.

Radio dispatch gave me a call to a housing project, a theft occurred at a women's apartment. Upon my arrival at the woman's apartment, I knocked on the door and was greeted by Mrs. Ruth who told me to follow her into the living room. Then Mrs. Ruth asked me to pull the sofa away from the wall which I did. Behind the wall was a large hole, big enough for a man to climb though with an extension cord which was sticking through the hole and plugged into Mrs. Ruth electric outlet. Mrs. Ruth said, "Look, my next door neighbors have been stealing electricity and climbing into her apartment and also stealing food."

I went next door to the neighbor's apartment and knocked on the door, several young children who were around 5 and 7 years old were very filthy. I asked the children where their parents were and they said, "Very sick." I came in the apartment and found the father sleeping on the couch and the mother was sleeping on the bed. Both parents were very filthy also and I could tell they were very sick by the way they were coughing and having a hard time standing up.

The father Leroy said, "It is my fault, take me to jail." We had no food or electricity so we stole it from the neighbor. I know what I did was wrong, but no one would help us and I had to take care of my family.

I called social services to help the family and housing maintenance fixed the wall. Mrs. Ruth decided not to press charges.

I got the other officers to chip in a couple of dollars and I bought some food for the family. Then I placed a call to the electric company and they turned the electric back onto the apartment.

Karma (sweepstakes) was good to me and I passed it on!

Chapter Twenty

Seven Finger Joe

The next day I received a call about a man with a cut hand. I responded with the paramedics and upon my arrival - I saw a man sitting on his front porch with a towel wrapped around his right hand. My sergeant told me to go inside of Mr. Joe Ts home and search for his missing fingers so they could be reattached later at the hospital. The paramedic quickly took Mr. Joe T. to the hospital and I rushed into the home looking for his fingers. I turned on some lights inside the home and discovered a nude dead woman on her back in the middle of the kitchen floor.

The dead woman had been cut down the middle of her chest and stomach and there was a large hunting knife still in her chest. I called my sergeant and several police cars caught up to the ambulance and put the handcuff on Joe T's left wrist. One of the police officers stayed with Joe T. and the paramedics as they continued back to the hospital.

I wasn't able to find the fingers and made a detailed report of the incident. The crime scene techs and homicide detectives also came to Joe T.'s home. The city morgue department came to the scene and took the dead woman away. I went to the hospital with the homicide detectives to question the murder suspect Joe T.

Joe T. calmly told us that he picked up the dead woman at a local bar then took her back to his house and had sex with her. After the sex we both walked naked into the kitchen and I stabbed her with a hunting knife to see what her insides looked like. Joe T. then said, "After stabbing the unknown woman he laid her down on her back, sliced her open and began pulling her intestines out and accidentally sliced off three of his fingers because the blade of the knife was still facing him."

The medical examiner Linda B. found three fingers inside the body cavity. It was an open and shut case and Joe T. was convicted and sent to the state hospital for the criminally insane. Joe T. gave me a weird smile and yelled, "Slater - I'll see you soon!"

I was thinking; Oh Crap! Crazy Joe was going to see me when he gets out. Trust me you'll lose sleep over a situation like that. Unfortunately, Sergeant Mike saw Joe T. about three years later walking near a mall and drove right up to Joe T. and said, "What are you doing out of the hospital?" Joe T. stated that he was released for good behavior and he started laughing because the woman he's dating knows nothing of his past. Then Joe T. told the Sergeant maybe I'll see you again one day and tell Slater "Hi" for me. Then Joe T. walked away whistling and smiling.

All police calls are so different - like the time I was called to a nude strip club. Upon my arrival I was told by the bouncer that there was a fight going on.

I rushed in and saw 6 or 7 naked women fighting over one customer who was a big tipper. Cat fights can be fun, but dangerous since some of the ladies carry knives.

Chapter Twenty One

Fight to the Death

The next few nights were pretty slow which is always good because I do need time to do my sweepstakes. While other cops hang out at the coffee shop, I'm writing away at my sweepstakes and still have time to solve crime and other related problems.

On Friday of that same week, I received a call to a house about a stabbing. Upon my arrival I walked up to the front screen porch door which was on the side of the house. An African-American male around 6'1" 240 lbs in his 50's was inside the screen-in porch. The man came to the front door and said, "Come on in, I'm going to kill you just like I killed my teenage daughter." The suspect was holding a large butcher knife and motioned me to enter. I pulled my gun and told the suspect to drop the knife. The suspect refused to drop the knife so I called for backup and radio dispatch told me there was no one available.

So I got this idea. I told the suspect I would put away my gun if he would drop the knife. Then I told him we could wrestle and if I won he would go to jail and if he won he didn't have to go!

"Crap, did I just say that?" The suspect quickly agreed and said come on in; I'm going to kick your ass. The suspect backed up into his living room and then charged at me when I entered the room. I must tell you I fought my ass off and we tore his living room up. The suspect had pushed me onto a coffee table and I broke it as I fell. The suspect then jumped on me and we were trading punches, then the suspect started choking me as I was laying on my back with the suspect on top of me. I was attempting to pull his hands away from my throat, when I looked for a brief second to my right and saw the suspect's daughter laying near the kitchen floor with a large butcher knife sticking out of her chest with a pool of blood around her.

I reached for anything that I could hit the suspect with; I grabbed a leg of the coffee table and hit the suspect numerous times until he let me go. I then tripped the suspect and was able to get him on his stomach and handcuffed him. Damn! The fight took every once of energy out of me.

As I was escorting the suspect out of the house for some unknown reason he began to whistle. I just thought the suspect was nuts. Then just as I was about to open the rear driver's side door to put the suspect in the car, I was struck by an unknown force.

The unknown force turned out to be a 100 pound german shepherd which rammed me to the ground. While on the ground the suspect began kicking me even though he was handcuffed with his hands in the back.

I was trying to hold the mouth of the german shepherd shut so he could not bite my face or neck. Finally I struck the dog with my fist; I was able to stun the dog for a moment while I pushed the suspect into the car.

Then the dog attacked me again and I jumped on the trunk and slid across the trunk onto the other side of the car. The dog then jumped on the trunk. I jumped off the trunk and ran around and jumped onto the hood of the car - then slid across and jumped off and got into the driver's side door, the dog had jumped onto the hood of the car and would not get off.

I punched the gas and the dog went sailing over the top of the car. I could see the dog in the rear view mirror attempting to chase my police car. Homicide and crime scene techs came to the scene of the homicide and I took the suspect to jail. Then I went back to the house, animal control also arrived and took the dog away. The detectives saw the condition of the living room and said, "The daughter must have put up a great fight before she was killed."

My Sergeant came to the scene and asked me why my pants were ripped and I said, "That the suspect's dog had bit me." My Sergeant told me to shoot the dog next time something like that happens and get checked for rabies.

After doing my paperwork I attempted to find a nice quite location to do my sweepstakes.

I was driving down another dirt road in the middle of no where when I spotted a large bonfire, I turned my lights off to see who it was, just being noisy. As I got closer I saw around 20 people dressed in brown robes chanting something and waving their arms up in the air as they walked around the fire. Then I saw one person wearing a black robe with a large knife yelling something as he was raising his knife in a stabbing position.

On a table close to the fire was a small type of animal which they looked like they were going to kill. I yelled, "What's going on?" The large group scattered in many different directions. I went to the fire and there was a cat tied down on the table. I let it go and it jumped off the table - it turned around like it was thanking me then ran into the dark woods.

Then I heard a loud voice in the dark woods, saying you have no right being here and we will find the officer, driving police car #143. It really got spooky quiet and I jumped back into my police car and drove away. Now that's just great! I have crazy Joe & devil worshipers looking for me!

The next night while on routine patrol on a local highway, I was driving northbound when a motorcycle 300 yards in front of my police car crashed as it drove over a slick spot on the roadway. Since I was right behind him I turned on my emergency lights and stopped traffic. Luckily there was no incoming traffic at the moment.

I saw that the driver had his leg ripped off and I ran and got a piece of rope out of my trunk - I made a tourniquet to stop the bleeding. The paramedics quickly showed up which was good because the man was going into shock. The man's custom motorcycle was destroyed.

I wrote the accident report and didn't think much about it until about two months later, one night a group of 20 to 30 motorcycle gang members came roaring up to my police station. The gang was in a straight line and they stopped near the entrance of the police station and the leader of the gang was yelling out my name.

Meanwhile other police officers in the parking lot had quickly come into the station and were grabbing shotguns thinking we were about to have a shootout. My Sergeant heard the gang leader yelling out my name and asked who did I piss off? The other guys told me to go out and see what he wanted. I guess better to lose one officer than many others.

I knew that I hadn't pissed off anyone except crazy Joe & the devil worshipers so I was okay. It was a long walk to the motorcycle leader and trust me - I was sweating like a stuck pig.

The leader got off his motorcycle and approached me and I figured we were going to fight, but instead he bear hugged the crap out of me. The leader of the gang was name, "Jake." He told me that I saved their brother who was in their motorcycle club and he said, "If I ever needed their help, they would be there for me."

Afterwards Jake got back on his motorcycle and all the motorcycle guys slapped me a "High Five" as they drove by, leaving the police station. I sure did gain a lot of respect from my fellow officers and the guys would joke around and say don't get your motorcycle gang after us!

So the rest of my week went great and I rode with this one cop named Christopher who had a funny sense of humor. We were assigned a traffic accident and before we got there the traffic was very heavy and slow but we finally made it. Once we got to the accident scene, I started doing the paperwork and Christopher did the traffic control and helped the paramedic's out.

One of the paramedic's told Christopher that inside the plastic bag was the decapitated head of the driver in vehicle one. So Christopher peeks inside the bag and sees the head of a white male around 30 years old. The traffic was moving very slowly and Christopher heard an older woman in her 60's yelling at her husband to slow down so she could see the accident. Christopher gets the bright idea of pulling the decapitated head out of the bag and showed the old woman. The woman immediately passed out. The husband of the woman who passed out called the police station and our sergeant yelled at us when we got back to the police station. I got in trouble for not stopping Christopher from doing something stupid.

Later that day Christopher and I had several court cases that were being heard by the local judge. There were several other police officers also having their court cases heard so we had to wait. While waiting for our case to be heard, the judge asked a white male in his 40's to stand up and be sworn in which he did. The judge asked the defendant if what the officer reported was true and the defendant screamed, "You're damn right I screwed my dog." And the courtroom went crazy with laughter. The judge was slamming down his gavel and said, "Order, Order!"

The defendant screamed the dog is my bitch and I will fuck her if I want to!"

The Judge said, "Take this defendant away." The courtroom was still laughing.

Chapter Twenty Two

The Devil Made Me Do It!

I had the Friday after Thanksgiving off and was just watching T.V. around 10:00 pm at night when I heard dogs barking in my front yard. Well! I thought this was strange since I didn't own dogs and neither did my neighbors. So I went outside to see what was going on.

There was a large white delivery envelope in the middle of my front door. So I opened it, thinking it was some type of sweepstakes trip or cash - since the sweepstakes normally mails those types of sweepstakes as certified mail.

Well I couldn't believe it - I finally won the BIG ONE! I won "One Million Dollars" payable at $40,000.00 a year for 25 years. WOW! I was in shock and I called my family and friends who soon after, wanted to start doing sweepstakes themselves.

Well the party time is over and I went back to work. I was working the daylight shift which was 8:00 am to 4:00 pm. The day was quiet until I received a phone harassment police call.

The victim was a woman at Oak Meadow apartment complex, Apartment #1307. Upon my arrival I knocked on the door and I heard a man say, "Who is it?" I answered, "The police." Well, this went on for several minutes trying to get the caller to the front door. Finally the man opened the front door and he had his right hand behind his back and I said, "I need to see both hands when I talk with someone."

After asking the man several times; "What's in your other hand," he all of a sudden whipped around the hand that was behind his back and pointed a gun to my forehead.

I took immediate action by swinging my body sideways and pushed the gun in the opposite direction. The suspect then slammed the door. I wasn't sure I had a hostage situation - since there was suppose to be a woman home. Swat came to the location and was able to arrest the man after breaking down the door. The man was so big they needed two pairs of handcuffs.

I searched the apartment and found the owner of the apartment tied up in the bedroom closet. The perpetrator was the ex-boyfriend of the victim. I went to court and the perpetrator was charged with burglary, kidnapping and attempted murder on a law enforcement officer.

The judge asked the defendant if he was going to shoot and he said, "Yes! That the "Satan" told him to shoot Officer Slater."

Wow! I go from winning a million dollars to almost getting shot in the head!

The last police call of the day was a death by heart attack. I arrived at the caller's location and was met by Susan S. who said, "Her father was dead and had a massive heart attack while on the toilet."

I followed Susan S. to the back of the house where there were 5 or 6 people standing outside a bathroom. I looked inside the bathroom and saw Robert S. buck-naked with his ass sticking straight up in the air.

I asked for someone to get me a sheet to cover Robert S. As I was doing this, a guy named Joe B. who was Robert S's. Brother-in-law - was in the bedroom looking through Robert S's. wallet.

I asked him, "Sir, what are you doing?" Joe B. stated that Robert S. owed him money and he was taking it. I said, "No, you're not, have respect for the dead."

Chapter Twenty Three

New Year's Eve

The night was already very busy with all the New Year's celebrating going on! At 11:00 pm

I started patrolling the west side of police sector 3 and came across a suspicious African-American male around 30 year old driving a 4 door sedan with its headlights off.

The suspect was driving at a high rate of speed and I began to follow him and check the license plate through the police computer system and it came back stolen. I advised police radio that I was going to pull over this stolen car and then as I turned my emergency lights on, the suspect took off and the chase was on!

The chase was going in and around numerous side streets until the suspect decided to crash in a century old graveyard's black wrought iron fence. The suspect then jumped out and started running in the graveyard.

I was running quickly behind the suspect until I caught up with him and was able to tackle him. I guess the weight of both of us hitting the ground at the same time caused the old graveyard ground to give way sending us both straight down onto a very old coffin.

The suspect landed on top of the coffin which broke apart sending him into a decaying corpse with me following on top of the suspect, jammed and stuck below ground level.

So now the suspect is screaming because he was terrified on top of this rotting corpse. I finally managed to get us both of us out of the graveyard hole. I took the suspect to the jail and he still continued to scream and he told me that the corpse was moving - in his mind he thought the corpse was going to drag him to hell.

It was a very funny night! It was an exciting police career and I ended up retiring several months later. I didn't find any buried treasure in the house that we grew up in, but I did find my "Pot of Gold" in the Sweepstakes!!!!

The End

Michael C. Slater

~~————————~~, ...

Dear Prizewinner,

Reference is made to the ⌐   uiiuiiui ....
and the prize you have won of a $1,000,000.00 non-transferable annuity to be paid in equal
annual installments of $40,000.00 each for 25 years without interest.

We are enclosing a check in the amount of $40,000.00 which represents the first installment of
this prize. You will be receiving additional information, pertaining to the annuity, from our
client in the near future.

May we remind you that our client is legally required to file a statement with the
                          e concerning this prize. The same responsibility is incumbent upon the
prize winner.

On behalf of our client, we thank you for your participation in this game and hope that you will
enjoy this prize.

Cordially,

       0   Jl   l .

e &   u.

encl.

FORTY THOUSAND AND 00/100 DOLLARS

DATE 12/18/2001 CHECK AMOUNT ***********40,000.00

MICHAEL C. SLATER

AUTHORIZED SIGNATURE

	VENDOR NO.			VENDOR NAME	
	MICSLA			MICHAEL C. SLATER	

TRANSACTION DATE	REFERENCE	GROSS AMOUNT	DEDUCTION	NET AMOUNT
2/01/2001	120346	40000.00	.00	40000.00
	9721			

CHECK DATE	CHECK NO.	TOTAL GROSS	TOTAL DEDUCTION	CHECK AMOUNT
2/18/2001	0018245	40000.00	.00	40000.00

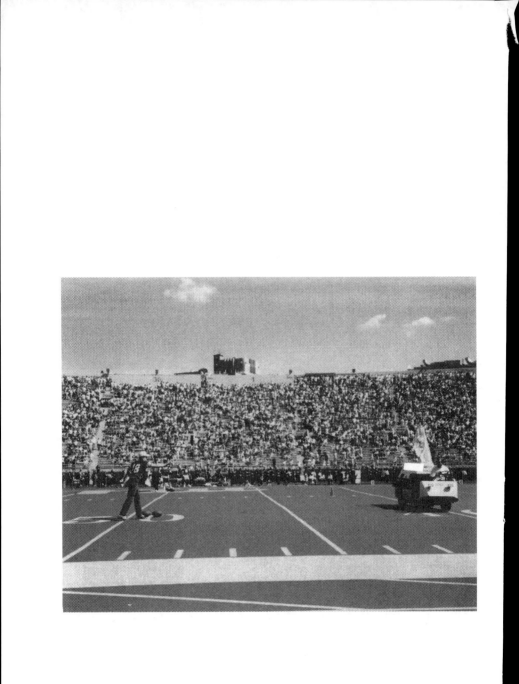

Printed in the United States
By Bookmasters